LABYRINTH OF ABYSS

BOOK 1

Y.K.R.

For those who find themselves navigating through the labyrinth of life, may this story serve as a reminder that even in the darkest of times, there is light to be found. To my loved ones, whose unwavering support sustains me through every twist and turn, and to the readers who embark on this journey with open hearts, this book is dedicated to you.

"Darkness cannot drive out darkness; only light can do that. Hate cannot drive out hate; only love can do that." - Martin Luther King Jr.

Contents

Foreword — vii

Preface — ix

Acknowledgements — xi

Prologue — xiii

1. Into The Abyss — 1

2. Forgotten Memories — 3

3. The Enigma Revealed — 7

4. Paths Of Peril — 10

5. Cryptic Messages — 12

6. Betrayal In The Shadows — 15

7. Echoes Of The Past — 18

8. Trails Of Trust — 20

9. Descent Into Darkness — 23

10. The Heart Of The Maze — 25

11. Revelations Unveiled — 27

12. Alliance Fractured — 29

13. Labyrinth Of Lies — 31

14. Race Against Time — 33

15. The Final Confrontation — 37

16. Beyond The Walls — 42

17. The Viral Plague — 51

The FORBIDDEN ODYSSEY — 55

Foreword

In "Labyrinth of the Abyss," readers will embark on a gripping adventure through a world forever changed by the aftermath of an apocalyptic virus. As our characters navigate the treacherous corridors of an ancient labyrinth, they will confront challenges, unravel mysteries, and forge bonds that transcend the darkness surrounding them.

Set against a backdrop of uncertainty and danger, this tale explores themes of survival, friendship, and the resilience of the human spirit. Through the eyes of Ethan, Ava, Liam, and Maya, readers will discover the power of hope in the face of adversity and the importance of standing together in times of peril.

As you delve into the depths of the labyrinth alongside our characters, prepare to be immersed in a world filled with twists, turns, and unexpected revelations. "Labyrinth of the Abyss" is a testament to the strength of the human spirit and the enduring power of friendship in the darkest of times.

Let the journey begin...

Preface

"Labyrinth of the Abyss" is a story that emerged from the depths of imagination, born from a desire to explore themes of resilience, friendship, and the human capacity for survival in the face of adversity. Set in a world shattered by the aftermath of an apocalyptic virus, this tale takes readers on a journey through the twisting corridors of an ancient labyrinth, where secrets lie buried and dangers lurk in the shadows.

As you turn the pages of this book, prepare to be immersed in a world teeming with mystery, intrigue, and unexpected twists. Through the eyes of our characters—Ethan, Ava, Liam, and Maya—you will experience the highs and lows of their journey, as they navigate through the labyrinth in search of answers and hope.

While "Labyrinth of the Abyss" is a work of fiction, it is my hope that its themes resonate with readers on a deeper level, reminding us all of the resilience of the human spirit and the importance of standing together in times of crisis. May this story serve as a beacon of light in the darkness, offering solace and inspiration to those who find themselves lost in the labyrinth of life.

With gratitude and anticipation,

Y.K.R.

Acknowledgements

I am deeply grateful to those who have supported me throughout the journey of creating "Labyrinth of the Abyss."

First and foremost, I would like to thank my family for their unwavering encouragement and understanding during the writing process. Your love and support have been my anchor through the highs and lows of this creative endeavor.

I extend my heartfelt appreciation to my friends and beta readers for their invaluable feedback and constructive criticism. Your insights have helped shape this story into what it is today.

A special thank you to my editor for their dedication and expertise in polishing the manuscript to its finest form.

I am indebted to the entire publishing team for their hard work and dedication in bringing "Labyrinth of the Abyss" to life.

Lastly, I extend my deepest gratitude to the readers who embark on this journey with Ethan, Ava, Liam, and Maya. Your enthusiasm and support mean the world to me.

Thank you all for being a part of this incredible adventure.

Y.K.R

Prologue

All he could only see were bluish white ghostly figures of humans,due to the blue lights reflecting their white coats, in front of him in a chamber, maybe a laboratory more like an operation theater? He questioned his mind. His senses were almost un functionable only his eyes and ears were working but it seemed like the eyes would stop working. He was looking towards his feet and saw the gate on which a red light was blinking. At last all he could see was darkness, then he sighed deeply.

Soon he hears a female's voice echoing, " everything is fine... just bring a revolution..."

He could hear the clicking of buttons and pulling of levers.

The same female voice echoes again in his mind, "Here it goes... Gen7-Subject#24"

And she repeats, "Everything is fine..."

Later all he could hear was a sound like ten formula 1 cars driving together at the same acceleration.

His eyes opened and find himself sleeping on a platform, he quickly stands up, cleans the dust on his sleeves and notices that he's in a dusty elevator with metallic walls and the roof of the elevator there were five lights placed on its roof which reflected the dust particles making them looking like fireflies acting like the moon.

He was totally confused where he was, later he heard some noise of machines functioning which was hurting his ears.

He thought he was trapped in a factory, he concluded by the noise and dust. Slowly he was losing his memory due to high noise pollution , all he could see were the hallucinations of the remaining memory, even his name and his brain started hurting from all the hallucinations he saw which was painful so he crouched down on his knees and then put his elbow on the platform and his whole body was shivering and his saliva was pouring out from his mouth.

He put his head down with a shock and fell on the platform he was standing on.

Later he heard a deep voice in his final hallucination saying, "Ethan, Wake up to reality, Ethan".

He uttered, "Ethan.. wait... Ethan.".

Now he remembered his own name and soon his headache was over but he lost the rest of the memory , he attempted to stand up and he was successful.

Soon the lift went down which seemed strange to Ethan, he looked up and took a deep breath.

Gradually gathering speed the lift was going up, at one time, the lift was so fast that it felt like traveling on an airplane without fastening his seat belt.

The lift was moving too fast for Ethan that he started screaming and hold the walls of the elevator but the elevator was going faster than Ethan thought that he finally fell on the ground and the platform separated from the elevator and fell down, so did Ethan, from him the time freezed like everything was going slow, now the dust particles looked like a cloud forming over his face by which he was dropping like a raindrop.

Ethan saw himself falling down in an endless void by a cuboid tunnel with wires and pipes on its walls.

He tried to catch a particle of dust but the time became normal and fall down at a high speed and he screamed but it was of no use.

At last he fell down on the ground but he was unhurt, he stood up holding his right elbow and found himself in a maze-like thing wi

th high walls and darkness.

CHAPTER ONE

INTO THE ABYSS

The darkness was suffocating as Ethan stumbled forward, his heart pounding in his chest. He could hear the echoing footsteps of his companions somewhere ahead, but the labyrinthine corridors seemed to swallow their voices, leaving him feeling utterly alone.

With each step, memories flickered at the edge of his consciousness—fragments of a life he couldn't quite grasp. But there was no time to dwell on the past, not when survival depended on finding a way out of this maze.

A sudden clang echoed through the darkness, causing Ethan to freeze in his tracks. Ahead, a faint glimmer of light danced tantalizingly, drawing him forward like a moth to flame. Ignoring the warning bells ringing in his mind, he quickened his pace, desperate to reach the source of illumination.

As he rounded a corner, the corridor opened up into a vast chamber, its walls adorned with cryptic symbols and faded murals. In the center of the room stood a towering structure—a massive door adorned with intricate carvings and pulsating with an otherworldly energy.

Ethan's breath caught in his throat as he approached, his hand reaching out to touch the pulsating surface. Before he could make contact, however, a voice echoed through the chamber, sending shivers down his spine.

"Welcome, travelers," it intoned, its tone both welcoming and ominous. "You have entered the realm of the Enigma, where truth lies hidden and challenges abound. But beware, for not all who enter these walls will emerge unscathed."

With a sinking feeling in the pit of his stomach, Ethan turned to see his companions emerging from the shadows, their faces a mixture of fear and determination. Together, they stood before the enigmatic door, ready to face whatever lay beyond as they embarked on their journey into t

he abyss.

CHAPTER TWO

FORGOTTEN MEMORIES

They introduced each other for others, Ethan looked like a 16 year old with dark and slight unkempt hairs giving him a rugged appearance, Intense, piercing eyes that reflect his determination and inner strength.

Strong jawline, adding to his overall sense of resilience and determination.

Athletic build, suggesting that he is physically capable and active in navigating the challenges of the labyrinth. Scars or other physical markers of the trials he has endured, serving as a reminder of his resilience and courage.

He came and meet the other team members, the first he meet was Ava, a girl having Long, flowing hair, perhaps blonde or brunette, symbolizing her grace and elegance.

Soft, expressive eyes that convey intelligence and depth.

Delicate features, including a slender nose and high cheekbones, giving her a refined appearance.

Tall and slender stature, with a graceful posture that commands attention.

A warm, inviting smile that puts others at ease and reflects her compassionate nature.

Perhaps bearing a scar or two from previous challenges, serving as a reminder of her resilience and inner strength.

Second he meet was Liam who had a Muscular build, suggesting strength and athleticism from navigating through the challenges of the labyrinth.

Short, cropped hair or a rugged hairstyle, reflecting his practical nature and readiness for action.

Piercing eyes with a determined gaze, indicating his unwavering resolve and determination to overcome obstacles.

Square jawline and stubbled chin, adding to his rugged and masculine appearance.

Tall stature, giving him a commanding presence among the group.

Scars or battle wounds, serving as a testament to his bravery and resilience in the face of danger.

Third was Jacob, who was dark skinned and muscular, with dark short crew cut hair wearing a pale-white t shirt and green cargo pant.

Fourth was Maya, who had Dark, flowing hair, perhaps with a hint of waves or curls,

Almond-shaped eyes, deep and expressive, reflecting her inner strength and resilience.

Sharp features, including high cheekbones and a defined jawline, giving her a striking and memorable appearance.

Medium height, with a slender yet toned physique that suggests agility and grace.

Delicate yet determined expression, hinting at the complexities of her character and her ability to navigate through challenges with confidence.

Perhaps bearing a few scars or marks from past encounters, adding to her aura of mystery and intrigue.

And the last one, Mia, she had a symmetrical face with high cheekbones, a slender nose, and lips that curve into a subtle smile. Her dark hair cascades in loose waves around her shoulders, framing her face with an air of mystery and allure. Her eyes are piercing, holding a universe of emotions, and her presence exudes quiet strength and resilience.

They asked Ethan that what was his stone?

"What stone are you all talking about?" Asked Ethan.

"The stone of roles... I got a green which means a defender, Ava got white which means a guide, Mia got red that is of a Medic and Mia got orage for a inventor... What about you Jacob?" Said Liam.

"Ha, No doubt I will get the Blue one!" Replied Jacob.

"You mean this?" Said Ethan holding the Blue stone. Everyone shocked after seeing Ethan having the blue one, it was of team leader.

"Impossible! I am more stronger." Said Jacob. When he looked at his pocket, he got the green one.

"You can't do anything, it is written in the scriptures, you have to obey the rules." Said Ava.

"What rules?" Asked Ethan, then Ava pointed towards the wall on which some encrypted signs on it.

As the echoes of the mysterious voice faded into the darkness, the group stood in stunned silence, their minds reeling with questions and uncertainty. Ethan's gaze swept over his companions, each one grappling with their own inner turmoil.

"We need to keep moving," Ethan finally declared, his voice firm despite the lingering unease in his gut. "We can't afford to stay stagnant in this place."

With reluctant nods, the group set off once more, their footsteps echoing through the labyrinthine corridors. As they walked, fragments of memories continued to flicker at the edge of Ethan's consciousness, teasing him with glimpses of a life long forgotten.

He saw flashes of laughter and warmth, of faces he couldn't quite place and places he couldn't quite remember. But the harder he tried to grasp onto them, the more they slipped through his fingers like grains of sand.

"We have to find a way out of here," Ava's voice broke through his reverie, pulling him back to the present. "We can't let this maze consume us."

Ethan nodded in agreement, his mind racing with possibilities. But as they pressed forward, each corridor seemed to lead to yet another dead end, leaving them no closer to uncovering the labyrinth's secrets.

Hours passed in a blur of uncertainty and fear, until finally, they stumbled upon a small alcove hidden away in the shadows. Within it lay a tattered journal, its pages yellowed with age and filled with cryptic writings written by the people who came before them.

"This could be a clue," Maya murmured, her fingers tracing the faded ink. "Perhaps it holds the key to unlocking the maze."

With bated breath, the group gathered around as Maya began to decipher the ancient text, her voice filling the silence with hope and determination. And as the words of the journal danced before their eyes, Ethan felt a glimmer of something stir within him—a sense of purpose, of destiny waiting to be fulfilled.

For in that moment, he knew that their journey was only just beginning, and that the mysteries of the Enigma were far from being unraveled. But with each step they took, they grew one step closer to uncovering the truth and reclaiming the memories that lay hidden within the l

abyrinth's depths.

CHAPTER THREE

THE ENIGMA REVEALED

As the group ventured deeper into the labyrinth, the oppressive weight of uncertainty hung heavy in the air. With each step forward, Ethan couldn't shake the feeling that they were being watched, as if unseen eyes followed their every move from the shadows.

The corridors twisted and turned, leading them further into the heart of the maze, where the very walls seemed to pulsate with an otherworldly energy. Despite the growing sense of unease, the group pressed on, driven by an insatiable curiosity to uncover the secrets that lay hidden within the labyrinth's depths.

Their journey led them to a vast chamber unlike any they had encountered before—a cavernous space filled with strange machinery and humming with power. Ava's eyes widened in awe as she surveyed the room, her fingers tracing the intricate patterns etched into the walls the pattern was Head Control written in sort-of bad hand writing engraved on the wall and a symbol which seems like the main control.

"It's a control room," she breathed, her voice barely above a whisper. "But what is it controlling?"

Before anyone could answer, the walls of the chamber began to shimmer and shift, revealing a holographic display that bathed the room in an ethereal glow. Images flickered to life before their eyes, painting a vivid portrait of a world long forgotten—a world torn apart by war and chaos.

"This is the past," Maya murmured, her voice tinged with reverence. "But what does it have to do with us?"

As they watched in silence, the holographic display shifted once more, revealing a figure shrouded in darkness—a figure that seemed to be watching them from beyond the confines of the labyrinth.

"You have been chosen," a voice echoed through the chamber, its words sending shivers down Ethan's spine. "Chosen to unlock the secrets of the Enigma and restore balance to the world."

The weight of those words hung heavy in the air, stirring something deep within Ethan's soul. He could feel the weight of destiny pressing down upon him, urging him forward on a path he had only just begun to comprehend.

Suddenly Ethan saw a figure who was watching them from the darkness, out of curiosity he swiftly moved forward towards the figure and slowly gaining speed, he ran towards it, his teammates especially Ava told him to stop but he ignored them. As he reached it, it suddenly faded into the darkness and Ethan stood stunned.

When he looked back to his team, they were shouting to come back, some moments later he got to know that the walls were shifting and he was soon going to be sandwiched between the walls, so he sprint as fast as he could and was successful to reach the team and he rolled on the floor as he used his strength in sprinting.

Ethan looked back and saw the walls being collapsed, later Liam bends down and whispers to Ethan, "You would die a mosquito's death."

Ethan's face turns towards Liam and then Liam moves backwards and Ethan stands up.

But as they prepared to embark on the next leg of their journey, Ethan couldn't shake the feeling that their true purpose had yet to be revealed, and that the mysteries of the Enigma ran deeper than they could ever imagine. With each passing moment, the labyrinth seemed to come alive around them, whispering secrets that begged to be unraveled. And as the group set out once more into the

unknown, they knew that their que
st had only just begun.

CHAPTER FOUR

PATHS OF PERIL

As the group emerged from the chamber of revelations, their minds buzzed with questions and their hearts pounded with a newfound sense of purpose. The labyrinth stretched out before them like a vast, tangled web of possibilities, each path leading to unknown dangers and untold secrets.

Ethan took the lead, his eyes scanning the twisting corridors for any sign of danger. But no matter which direction they turned, the maze seemed to shift and change around them, confounding their efforts to find a way out.

Hours turned into days as they pressed forward, their journey fraught with peril at every turn. They encountered deadly traps and cunning puzzles, each one testing their wits and their resolve. But with each obstacle they overcame, their bond grew stronger, forging them into a cohesive unit capable of facing any challenge.

Yet amidst the trials and tribulations of their journey, tensions began to simmer beneath the surface, threatening to tear the group apart. Ava and Maya clashed over strategy, their differing viewpoints causing friction within the ranks, Ethan tried to stop them but they ignored him like he didn't exist. Liam grew increasingly reckless, his thirst for adventure putting the group in ever-greater danger. And Ethan found himself struggling to hold the group together, his leadership tested like never before.

But even as their unity wavered, they pressed on, driven by a shared sense of purpose and a determination to uncover the truth.

And as they journeyed deeper into the labyrinth, they began to sense that they were drawing closer to their goal—that somewhere amidst the twisting corridors and hidden passages lay the key to unlocking the mysteries of the Enigma.

As they reached a particularly treacherous section of the maze, Ethan paused, his gaze sweeping over his companions with a mixture of determination and apprehension.

"We may be lost in this maze," he declared, his voice echoing through the darkness, "but as long as we stand together, we will find our way out."

With renewed resolve, the group pressed forward, their footsteps echoing through the labyrinth as they ventured ever deeper into the heart of the Enigma. And though the path ahead was fraught with peril, they knew that their journey was far from over—and that the greatest challenges

still lay ahead.

CHAPTER FIVE

CRYPTIC MESSAGES

The group's journey through the labyrinth was fraught with tension and uncertainty, each step forward revealing new challenges and mysteries. As they ventured deeper into the heart of the Enigma, the air grew thick with anticipation, every shadow seeming to hide a potential threat.

Their progress was slow and methodical, the maze twisting and turning in on itself like a tangled web of confusion. Ethan led the way, his senses alert for any sign of danger, while Ava and Maya analyzed the cryptic messages that adorned the walls, searching for clues to their whereabouts.

Hours passed as they deciphered the ancient writings, the group huddled together in the dim light of their torches, their minds racing with possibilities. With each new revelation, they felt a glimmer of hope—a sense that they were drawing closer to uncovering the truth behind the Enigma.

But danger lurked around every corner, and the group soon found themselves facing their most perilous challenge yet—a chamber filled with deadly traps and cunning puzzles. The chamber has 5 levels of trap, first was a pit which led to endless void, second was rain of dense and hot magma which could come any time, third was random arrow shooting from an ancient statue like dispenser, fourth was tile mines in which mines were placed on random tiles and fifth was wall of spike in which a spike will come out of random holes on the wall. But Ava's strategic brilliance guided them, they navigated the treacherous obstacles with skill and determination, their bond as a team growing stronger with each passing moment.

For the first level: Ava told the team to pull out their knives out of their bag to climb the wall and reach the vines that grew up there.

For the second: the only thing that came in Ava's mind and agreed by Ethan was "RUSH TO THE OTHER END, AS SOON AS POSSIBLE!" and everyone succeeded in it.

For the third: Ethan whispers to Ava, "Now what?"

"These arrows are going in a random pattern, there seems no guarantee."

Ethan sighed, but till then Ava claimed, "There seems only one way...".

Ethan turned his sight towards Ava, he didn't knew what's up to her,

She told Ethan to hold his bag on his left and Ava held her bag to her right and they held each other firmly and said "like last time..."

"RUN!" screamed both and succeeded to reach level 4. Ava gave a sign to call the other people of the team.

After everyone made it to the end, now it was time for...

Level 4: now it was the tile mines, Ava lost hope to make it. After telling the news other teammates also lost their hope and Liam became angry and started punching the wall and the wall broke into large pieces, then Mia got an idea which was to throw the pieces to deactivate the mines. According to Mia's plan they threw the largest piece and after the throw, they lied down and they crossed level 4.

Level 5: a deep voice came from nowhere saying, "Congratulations, you crossed all the 4 levels now it is the last level and don't be overconfident it might result in your end." everyone gasped after hearing it. Ava tried to study the pattern of the coming spikes but the spikes were coming in random patterns but there was less chance of spikes coming so they use the holes to climb the wall, they did face some challenges but they made it.

As they emerged victorious from the chamber, their hearts pounding with adrenaline, Ethan couldn't help but marvel at the resilience of his companions. Together, they had faced down impossible odds and emerged triumphant, their spirits unbroken despite the dangers that surrounded them.

Yet even as they celebrated their victory, a sense of foreboding lingered in the air. They knew that the Enigma held many more secrets, each one more elusive than the last. And as they prepared to press onward into the unknown, Ethan couldn't shake the feeling that their journey was far from over—that the true challenges still lay ahead, waiting to test their courage an

d resolve to the limit.

CHAPTER SIX

BETRAYAL IN THE SHADOWS

As the group ventured deeper into the labyrinth, tensions simmered beneath the surface, threatening to tear apart the fragile bonds that held them together. Ethan could feel the weight of uncertainty pressing down upon them, each step forward bringing them closer to the heart of the Enigma—and closer to the truth.

Their progress had been slow and arduous, the maze seemingly endless in its complexity. But despite the obstacles they faced, Ethan refused to let doubt cloud his judgment. He was determined to lead his companions to safety, no matter the cost.

Yet as they pressed onward, a sense of unease settled over the group like a shroud. Ava and Maya clashed over strategy, their differing viewpoints sparking heated debates that threatened to fracture their unity, for the last time Ethan tried to stop them and like always they ignored him like he didn't exist, so he held his head with his right arm and said, "These girls... will never listen". Liam grew increasingly reckless, accidentally Nathan pressed a black square like button thing by which the walls opened like two doors opening and a huge wall came tilting towards them and slowly going down. Jacob ordered everyone to run, Ava and Maya left their work of decoding to run and save their lives, the wall was falling and the group ran. The wall came so near and they still did not reach enough distance to dodge it, Ava pushed Ethan and both fell on the ground, Ethan looked back to Ava and saw the wall had collided with the roof of the Enigma and rock chunks fell on the ground and everyone fell on the ground but fortunately everyone survived, this impulsive actions putting the group in ever-greater danger as chunks fell on their way. And Ethan found himself struggling to maintain control, his leadership tested by the mounting pressure of their journey.

But amidst the turmoil that surrounded them, a new threat emerged—a shadowy figure lurking in the darkness, their motives shrouded in mystery. Ethan couldn't shake the feeling that they were being watched, that unseen eyes followed their every move, waiting for the perfect moment to strike.

As they reached a particularly treacherous section of the maze, Ethan called for a halt, his senses alert for any sign of danger. But before he could react, chaos erupted in their midst—a trap sprung, a betrayal revealed.

Maya, the compassionate healer with a hidden agenda, stood before them, her eyes cold and calculating. Ethan felt a surge of disbelief and betrayal wash over him as he stared into her eyes, searching for any sign of remorse.

"You were working with them all along," Ethan accused, his voice thick with anger and betrayal. "You betrayed us."

Maya said nothing, her silence a damning confirmation of Ethan's worst fears. With a sinking feeling in the pit of his stomach, Ethan realized that they had been played—that Maya had been feeding information to their enemies, leading them into a trap from which there may be no escape.

As the reality of Maya's betrayal sank in, the group stood in stunned silence, their minds reeling with shock and disbelief. How could someone they had trusted turn against them so easily? And what other secrets lay hidden within the labyrinth's depths, waiting to be uncovered?

Liam became grumpy and pushed Maya later Ava claims him down,

With Maya's true allegiance revealed, the group knew that they could no longer afford to trust blindly. They would need to be vigilant, to watch each other's backs as they navigated the treacherous maze of the Enigma. For amidst the shadows lurked dangers beyond imagining, and only by staying united could they hope to overcome the challe

nges that lay ahead

CHAPTER SEVEN

ECHOES OF THE PAST

The betrayal hung heavy in the air as the group grappled with the shocking revelation of Maya's true allegiance. Ethan's heart ached with a sense of betrayal and loss, his mind racing with questions he feared may never be answered.

As they retreated from the treacherous trap that Maya had led them into, a somber silence fell over the group. Each member was lost in their own thoughts, wrestling with the implications of Maya's betrayal and the dangers that now surrounded them.

But amidst the turmoil, a glimmer of determination flickered in Ethan's eyes. They couldn't afford to dwell on Maya's betrayal, not when their survival depended on staying focused and united. They needed to press forward, to uncover the truth behind the Enigma and find a way out of the labyrinth before it was too late.

With Ava's strategic mind guiding them, the group forged ahead, their footsteps echoing through the maze as they ventured deeper into its depths. Along the way, they encountered more cryptic messages and ancient symbols, each one a puzzle waiting to be solved.

As they deciphered the clues scattered throughout the labyrinth, Ethan couldn't shake the feeling that they were drawing closer to unlocking the secrets of the Enigma. But with Maya's betrayal still fresh in their minds, he couldn't help but wonder if there were other dangers lurking in the shadows, waiting to strike when they least expected it.

Yet despite the uncertainty that clouded their path, Ethan refused to let fear dictate their actions. They would face whatever challenges lay ahead with courage and determination, for they were bound by a common goal—to uncover the truth and escape the labyrinth's clutches once and for all. And as they ventured deeper into the heart of the Enigma, Ethan couldn't shake the feeling that their journey was far from over—that the echoes of the past still held secrets waiting to b

e revealed

CHAPTER EIGHT

TRAILS OF TRUST

As the group ventured deeper into the labyrinth, the weight of Maya's betrayal hung heavy in the air, casting a shadow over their every move. Ethan could feel the tension among them like a palpable force, each member grappling with their own sense of betrayal and uncertainty.

But amidst the turmoil, a sense of determination burned bright within Ethan's heart. They couldn't afford to let Maya's betrayal tear them apart, not when their survival depended on staying united. They needed to trust each other now more than ever, to rely on the strength of their bonds to see them through the challenges that lay ahead.

With Ava's strategic mind guiding them, the group pressed forward, their footsteps echoing through the maze as they navigated its treacherous corridors. Along the way.

Suddenly they heard a sound of a non- human walking on the top, Ethan stopped for a while and started scanning his surrounding, meanwhile something fell on Nathan's hairs, something slimy when Nathan took it on his hands then he got to know that it is thick and smells like burnt rubber, Ethan looked above Nathan but saw nothing. Ethan ordered to move forward.

As he moved ahead a gigantic monster appeared in front of him. It had six long legs like a spider, body like an ant, a face like a monkey with big teeth and its saliva pouring out from its mouth and a tail like a scorpion.

Everyone had an expression of courage and fear.

Courage to fight it and fear as they had no tool except a knife.

That thing banged its first two legs on the ground and the soil on ground molded into slug-like creatures but they moved fast unlike real slug and had eyes and tail like scorpion, the team took out the knife from their pockets, one of the slug jumped over Ethan's face but Ethan cut it in half before it arrived on its face, later it the team got the courage to fight those creatures and soon they defeated all the creatures but the spider thingy climbed the wall and gone, everyone cheered on their victory.

Despite the betrayal they had endured, they remained steadfast in their determination to uncover the truth and escape the labyrinth's clutches.

But even as they forged ahead, danger lurked around every corner, waiting to ensnare them in its deadly embrace. They again encountered those strange creatures lurking in the shadows, now their eyes glowing with malevolent intent. And with each passing moment, Ethan couldn't shake the feeling that they were being watched—that unseen eyes followed their every move, waiting for the perfect moment to strike.

Yet amidst the dangers that surrounded them, a sense of camaraderie flourished within the group. They supported each other through moments of doubt and fear, drawing strength from the bonds they had forged amidst the chaos of the labyrinth.

As they reached a particularly perilous section of the maze, Ethan called for a halt, his senses alert for any sign of danger. But before they could react, a deafening roar echoed through the corridors, signaling the approach of a deadly adversary. Later those strange creatures came, but now they surrounded them from all directions.

Now the group sprang into action, their weapons drawn and their minds focused on the task at hand,now the weapons were knives attached to vines and a cane which they got in the middle of their way and was made by Mia. Together, they faced the looming threat head-on, their trust in each other is their greatest weapon against the darkness that threatened to consume them.

And as they emerged victorious from the battle, their spirits lifted by their triumph over adversity, Ethan couldn't help but feel a sense of hope stirring within him. For amidst the trials of trust and the dangers that lurked in the shadows, he knew that as long as they stood united, they would find a way to overcome whateve
r challenges lay ahead.

CHAPTER NINE

DESCENT INTO DARKNESS

The labyrinth stretched before them like an endless maze of shadows and whispers, its corridors twisting and turning with malicious intent. Ethan led the group, his senses on high alert, every step forward a gamble in the game of survival they found themselves playing.

Maya's betrayal lingered like a bitter taste in Ethan's mouth, a constant reminder of the fragile trust that bound them together. He couldn't shake the feeling of betrayal, the nagging doubt that threatened to unravel the very fabric of their unity.

But amidst the turmoil, a sense of determination burned bright within Ethan's heart. They couldn't afford to let Maya's betrayal tear them apart, not when their survival depended on staying united. They needed to trust each other now more than ever, to rely on the strength of their bonds to see them through the challenges that lay ahead.

With Ava's strategic guidance leading the way, they pressed forward, their steps echoing through the maze's twisting corridors. Liam's jaw clenched in determination, his eyes scanning the shadows for any sign of danger. Maya walked with her head bowed, her once warm demeanor now cloaked in silence and remorse.

Ethan found himself grappling with conflicting emotions—anger at Maya's betrayal, but also a flicker of empathy for the pain she must be enduring. He longed to confront her, to demand answers, but now was not the time for reckoning. Their survival depended on unity.

As they navigated through the labyrinth, they encountered increasingly treacherous obstacles. Deadly traps lay in wait, triggered by the slightest misstep. Jacob's keen instincts proved invaluable as he detected hidden pitfalls and snares, guiding the group safely through the dangers.

Yet, the darkness seemed to seep into their souls with each passing hour, wearing down their spirits like relentless waves crashing against the shore. Doubt gnawed at their resolve, threatening to fracture their unity.

But amidst the encroaching shadows, glimmers of hope pierced through the gloom. Ethan's leadership inspired courage in his companions, forging an unbreakable bond that defied the darkness. Sofia's ingenuity shone bright as she devised clever solutions to navigate the maze's traps, her quick thinking saving them from certain peril.

As they ventured deeper into the heart of the Enigma, Ethan felt a sense of foreboding grip his heart. The labyrinth seemed to grow ever more sinister, its walls closing in around them like a vice. Yet, he refused to succumb to despair.

With Ava's strategic guidance and Liam's unwavering bravery, they pressed on, their determination unyielding. They knew that the path ahead would be fraught with danger, but they would face it together, their spirits unbroken by the shadows that threatened to consume them.

And as they descended further into darkness, Ethan clung to the hope that somewhere amidst the labyrinth's depths, they would find the light they so desperately sought. For in the darkest of times, it was unity, courage, and hope that would ultimately guid
e them to salvation.

CHAPTER TEN

THE HEART OF THE MAZE

As the group pressed deeper into the labyrinth, the air grew heavy with a sense of foreboding. Every step forward felt like a leap into the unknown, the walls of the maze closing in around them like a suffocating embrace. Yet, amidst the darkness, a flicker of hope burned bright within their hearts.

Ethan led the way, his determination unwavering despite the trials they had faced. Ava's strategic mind remained their guiding light, her keen intellect cutting through the labyrinth's mysteries with ease. Liam's bravery bolstered their spirits, his unwavering courage a beacon of strength in the face of uncertainty.

But as they ventured further into the heart of the maze, the challenges they faced grew ever more daunting. Deadly traps lay hidden around every corner, their mechanisms designed to test the limits of their endurance and wit. Yet, with each obstacle they overcame, their bond as a group grew stronger, forged in the crucible of adversity.

As they reached a particularly treacherous section of the labyrinth, Ethan called for a halt, his senses on high alert for any sign of danger. The walls seemed to pulse with a malevolent energy, their very presence a testament to the labyrinth's power.

"We must proceed with caution," Ethan cautioned, his voice barely above a whisper. "The heart of the maze lies ahead, and with it, the answers we seek."

With Ava's strategic guidance leading the way, they pressed forward, their footsteps echoing through the maze's twisting corridors. Maya walked beside Ethan, her gaze fixed on the path ahead, her once warm demeanor now cloaked in silence and remorse.

As they navigated through the darkness, a sense of unease settled over the group like a shroud. They couldn't shake the feeling that they were being watched, that unseen eyes followed their every move, waiting for the perfect moment to strike.

But amidst the encroaching shadows, glimmers of hope pierced through the gloom. Ethan's leadership inspired courage in his companions, forging an unbreakable bond that defied the darkness. Mia's ingenuity shone bright as she devised clever solutions to navigate the maze's traps, her quick thinking saving them from certain peril.

As they ventured deeper into the heart of the Enigma, Ethan felt a sense of foreboding grip his heart. The labyrinth seemed to grow ever more sinister, its walls closing in around them like a vice. Yet, he refused to succumb to despair.

With Ava's strategic guidance and Liam's unwavering bravery, they pressed on, their determination unyielding. They knew that the path ahead would be fraught with danger, but they would face it together, their spirits unbroken by the shadows that threatened to consume them.

And as they descended further into darkness, Ethan clung to the hope that somewhere amidst the labyrinth's depths, they would find the light they so desperately sought. For in the darkest of times, it was unity, courage, and hope that would ultimately guid

e them to salvation.

CHAPTER ELEVEN

REVELATIONS UNVEILED

As the group delved deeper into the labyrinth, the weight of Maya's betrayal hung heavy in the air, casting a pall over their every move. Ethan struggled to reconcile his feelings, torn between anger and a lingering sense of betrayal. But amidst the turmoil, a voice of reason emerged—Ava, with her strategic mind and unwavering determination to see them through.

Their progress through the maze was slow and methodical, the oppressive darkness seemingly closing in around them with each step. Liam's usual bravado waned in the face of the unknown, his confidence shaken by Maya's deception. Yet, he remained resolute, determined to prove himself worthy of the trust they had placed in him.

As they navigated through the labyrinth's twisting corridors, they encountered obstacles that tested their resolve like never before. Deadly traps lay in wait, their mechanisms cunningly designed to ensnare the unwary. But with Ava's guidance and Ethan's leadership, they managed to overcome each challenge, their bond as a group growing stronger with every victory.

Yet, despite their progress, doubts lingered in the shadows, threatening to tear apart the fragile unity they had worked so hard to maintain. Maya's betrayal had shaken them to their core, sowing seeds of mistrust that festered in the darkness of the maze.

As they reached a particularly treacherous section of the labyrinth, Ethan called for a halt, his gaze sweeping over his companions with a mixture of concern and determination. The air seemed to crackle with tension, each member of the group lost in their own thoughts, grappling with the weight of their shared burden.

"We cannot let Maya's betrayal divide us," Ethan declared, his voice echoing through the darkness. "We must stay united if we are to survive."

With Ava's strategic guidance leading the way, they pressed forward, their footsteps echoing through the maze's twisting corridors. Liam's resolve hardened, his determination to prove himself unwavering in the face of adversity. Maya walked beside Ethan, her gaze fixed on the path ahead, her once warm demeanor now clouded with regret.

As they ventured deeper into the heart of the Enigma, Ethan felt a sense of foreboding grip his heart. The labyrinth seemed to grow ever more menacing, its secrets hidden in the shadows, waiting to be uncovered. Yet, he refused to let fear dictate their actions. They would face whatever challenges lay ahead together, their spirits unbroken by the shadows that threatened to consume them.

And as they descended further into darkness, Ethan clung to the hope that somewhere amidst the labyrinth's depths, they would find the answers they sought—and emerge stronger, united in their resolve to overcome whatever tria

ls awaited them.

CHAPTER TWELVE

ALLIANCE FRACTURED

As the group ventured deeper into the labyrinth, the weight of their recent discord hung heavy in the air like a suffocating shroud, obscuring their path and clouding their minds. Ethan's thoughts churned with a mix of emotions, the wounds of betrayal still fresh and raw. But amidst the turmoil, a flicker of determination burned within him, a resolve to see their journey through to its end, no matter the obstacles they faced.

With Ava's strategic guidance lighting the way, they pressed forward, their footsteps echoing through the maze's winding corridors. Liam's usual bravado had waned, replaced by a steely determination, his eyes scanning the shadows for any sign of danger. The tension among them was palpable, a silent reminder of the fracture that had torn through their once-united alliance.

As they navigated the labyrinth's treacherous pathways, they encountered obstacles that tested their resolve like never before. Deadly traps lay in wait at every turn, their mechanisms cunningly designed to ensnare the unwary. But with Ava's sharp mind and Ethan's unwavering leadership, they navigated each challenge with a combination of skill, caution, and sheer determination.

Yet, despite their progress, doubts lingered in the shadows, threatening to fracture the fragile bonds that held them together. The recent discord had shaken their trust, leaving them all wondering if their alliance could withstand the trials ahead.

As they reached a particularly perilous section of the maze, Ethan called for a halt, his senses on high alert for any sign of danger. The air seemed to hum with a malevolent energy, the darkness pressing in around them like a suffocating blanket.

"We must proceed with caution," Ethan urged, his voice low but firm. "The heart of the maze lies ahead, and with it, the answers we seek."

With Ava's guidance leading the way, they pressed forward, their footsteps echoing through the maze's twisting corridors. The silence that hung between them was heavy with unspoken tension, each member of the group grappling with their own doubts and fears.

As they ventured deeper into the labyrinth's depths, the darkness seemed to grow ever more oppressive, its weight bearing down on them like a physical force. Ethan could feel the tension in the air, a palpable sense of unease that seemed to permeate their very souls.

But amidst the encroaching shadows, glimmers of hope pierced through the gloom. Ethan's determination inspired courage in his companions, their resolve strengthened by their shared purpose. Ava's strategic brilliance guided them through the maze's myriad challenges, her sharp mind cutting through the darkness like a beacon of light.

And as they descended further into the abyss, Ethan clung to the hope that somewhere amidst the labyrinth's depths, they would find the answers they sought. For in the darkest of times, it was unity, courage, and hope that would ultimately lead them to the truth—and to the light that awaited them b

eyond the shadows.

CHAPTER THIRTEEN

LABYRINTH OF LIES

As the group ventured deeper into the labyrinth, the weight of their recent discord hung heavy in the air like a suffocating shroud, obscuring their path and clouding their minds. Ethan's thoughts churned with a mix of emotions, the wounds of betrayal still fresh and raw. But amidst the turmoil, a flicker of determination burned within him, a resolve to see their journey through to its end, no matter the obstacles they faced.

With Ava's strategic guidance lighting the way, they pressed forward, their footsteps echoing through the maze's winding corridors. Liam's usual bravado had waned, replaced by a steely determination, his eyes scanning the shadows for any sign of danger. The tension among them was palpable, a silent reminder of the fracture that had torn through their once-united alliance.

As they navigated the labyrinth's treacherous pathways, they encountered obstacles that tested their resolve like never before. Deadly traps lay in wait at every turn, their mechanisms cunningly designed to ensnare the unwary. But with Ava's sharp mind and Ethan's unwavering leadership, they navigated each challenge with a combination of skill, caution, and sheer determination.

Yet, despite their progress, doubts lingered in the shadows, threatening to fracture the fragile bonds that held them together. The recent discord had shaken their trust, leaving them all wondering if their alliance could withstand the trials ahead.

As they reached a particularly perilous section of the maze, Ethan called for a halt, his senses on high alert for any sign of danger. The air seemed to hum with a malevolent energy, the darkness pressing in around them like a suffocating blanket.

"We must proceed with caution," Ethan urged, his voice low but firm. "The heart of the maze lies ahead, and with it, the answers we seek."

With Ava's guidance leading the way, they pressed forward, their footsteps echoing through the maze's twisting corridors. The silence that hung between them was heavy with unspoken tension, each member of the group grappling with their own doubts and fears.

As they ventured deeper into the labyrinth's depths, the darkness seemed to grow ever more oppressive, its weight bearing down on them like a physical force. Ethan could feel the tension in the air, a palpable sense of unease that seemed to permeate their very souls.

But amidst the encroaching shadows, glimmers of hope pierced through the gloom. Ethan's determination inspired courage in his companions, their resolve strengthened by their shared purpose. Ava's strategic brilliance guided them through the maze's myriad challenges, her sharp mind cutting through the darkness like a beacon of light.

And as they descended further into the abyss, Ethan clung to the hope that somewhere amidst the labyrinth's depths, they would find the answers they sought. For in the darkest of times, it was unity, courage, and hope that would ultimately lead them to the truth—and to the light that awaited them b

eyond the shadows.

RACE AGAINST TIME

The labyrinth seemed to stretch endlessly before them, a maze of twisting corridors and hidden dangers that threatened to consume them whole. With each step forward, Ethan could feel the weight of their mission pressing down on him like a leaden cloak. Time was running out, and the urgency of their quest weighed heavily on his mind.

With Ava's strategic guidance lighting the way, they pressed forward, their footsteps echoing through the maze's winding corridors. Liam's usual bravado had waned, replaced by a grim determination as he scanned the shadows for any sign of danger. Maya walked beside Ethan, her once warm demeanor now clouded with uncertainty.

As they navigated the labyrinth's treacherous pathways, they encountered obstacles that tested their resolve like never before. Deadly traps lay in wait at every turn, their mechanisms cunningly designed to ensnare the unwary. But with Ava's sharp mind and Ethan's unwavering leadership, they navigated each challenge with a combination of skill, caution, and sheer determination.

Yet, despite their progress, the ever-present sense of urgency gnawed at Ethan's insides like a ravenous beast. Time was slipping away, and with each passing moment, the shadow of failure loomed larger. They needed to find the answers they sought, and they needed to find them quickly.

As they reached a particularly perilous section of the maze, Ethan called for a halt, his senses on high alert for any sign of danger. The air seemed to crackle with tension, the darkness pressing in around them like a tangible force.

"We must proceed with caution," Ethan urged, his voice low but firm. "Every moment wasted brings us closer to failure."

With Ava's guidance leading the way, they pressed forward, their footsteps echoing through the maze's twisting corridors. The silence that hung between them was heavy with unspoken tension, each member of the group acutely aware of the ticking clock that governed their every move.

As they ventured deeper into the labyrinth's depths, the darkness seemed to grow ever more oppressive, its weight bearing down on them like a physical force. Ethan could feel the weight of their mission pressing down on him like a leaden cloak, each passing moment fueling his sense of urgency.

But amidst the encroaching shadows, glimmers of hope pierced through the gloom. Ethan's determination inspired courage in his companions, their resolve strengthened by their shared purpose. Ava's strategic brilliance guided them through the maze's myriad challenges, her sharp mind cutting through the darkness like a beacon of light.

And as they descended further into the abyss, Ethan clung to the hope that somewhere amidst the labyrinth's depths, they would find the answers they sought. For in the darkest of times, it was unity, courage, and hope that would ultimately lead them to the truth—and to the light that awaited them beyond the shadows.

But the labyrinth seemed intent on thwarting their progress at every turn, its twisting corridors and hidden traps serving as constant reminders of the dangers that lurked in the darkness. Time was their greatest enemy, ticking away with each passing moment, driving them ever onward in their race against the clock.

As they pressed forward, Ethan's mind raced with a flurry of thoughts and possibilities. What secrets lay hidden within the maze's depths? And what dark truths awaited them at its heart? The answers seemed tantalizingly close yet maddeningly elusive, like ghosts that danced just beyond their grasp.

With Ava's guidance lighting the way, they navigated the labyrinth's treacherous pathways with a sense of urgency that bordered on desperation. Liam's usual bravado had been replaced by a grim determination, his eyes scanning the shadows for any sign of danger. Maya walked beside Ethan, her once warm demeanor now clouded with uncertainty.

Every step forward felt like a gamble, a leap of faith into the unknown. Yet, they pressed on, driven by a sense of purpose that burned bright within their hearts. Failure was not an option, not when so much was at stake.

But as they ventured deeper into the maze's depths, the darkness seemed to close in around them like a vice, its oppressive weight bearing down on their shoulders. Ethan could feel the weight of their mission pressing down on him like a leaden cloak, each passing moment fueling his sense of urgency.

"We must keep moving," Ethan urged, his voice low but firm. "We cannot afford to waste any more time."

With Ava's guidance leading the way, they pressed forward, their footsteps echoing through the maze's twisting corridors. The silence that hung between them was heavy with unspoken tension, each member of the group acutely aware of the ticking clock that governed their every move.

But as they pushed deeper into the labyrinth's depths, the challenges they faced grew ever more perilous. Deadly traps lay in wait around every corner, their mechanisms designed to ensnare the unwary. Yet, with Ava's sharp mind and Ethan's unwavering leadership, they navigated each obstacle with a combination of skill and determination.

Yet, despite their progress, Ethan could feel the weight of their mission bearing down on him like a crushing weight. Time was slipping away, slipping through their fingers like grains of sand, and with each passing moment, the shadow of failure loomed larger.

"We must find a way to speed up our progress," Ethan said, his voice tinged with frustration. "We cannot afford to be delayed any longer."

With renewed determination, they pressed on, their pace quickening as they raced against the clock. Every second mattered, every minute lost bringing them closer to failure. The pressure was relentless, a constant weight that pressed down on them with each step forward.

But amidst the chaos

and uncertainty, a sense of unity emerged.

CHAPTER FIFTEEN

THE FINAL CONFRONTATION

The labyrinth stretched before them like a vast, twisting puzzle, its corridors shrouded in darkness and uncertainty. With each step forward, Ethan felt the weight of their journey pressing down on him like a leaden cloak. They had come so far, faced countless trials and tribulations, and now, they stood on the brink of the final confrontation.

With Ava's strategic guidance lighting the way, they pressed forward, their footsteps echoing through the maze's winding corridors. Liam's usual bravado had been replaced by a grim determination, his eyes scanning the shadows for any sign of danger. Maya walked beside Ethan, her once warm demeanor now clouded with uncertainty.

As they navigated the labyrinth's treacherous pathways, they encountered obstacles that tested their resolve like never before. Deadly traps lay in wait at every turn, their mechanisms cunningly designed to ensnare the unwary. But with Ava's sharp mind and Ethan's unwavering leadership, they navigated each challenge with a combination of skill, caution, and sheer determination.

Yet, despite their progress, Ethan could feel the weight of their mission bearing down on him like a crushing weight. Time was slipping away, slipping through their fingers like grains of sand, and with each passing moment, the shadow of failure loomed larger.

"We must find a way to speed up our progress," Ethan said, his voice tinged with frustration. "We cannot afford to be delayed any longer."

With renewed determination, they pressed on, their pace quickening as they raced against the clock. Every second mattered, every minute lost bringing them closer to failure. The pressure was relentless, a constant weight that pressed down on them with each step forward.

But amidst the chaos and uncertainty, a sense of unity emerged among them. They had faced countless trials together, overcome insurmountable odds, and now, they stood united in their determination to see their mission through to its end.

As they ventured deeper into the heart of the labyrinth, the air seemed to crackle with tension, the darkness pressing in around them like a tangible force. Ethan could feel the weight of their mission bearing down on him, a sense of urgency driving him forward with each step.

"We're getting closer," Ava said, her voice filled with quiet determination. "I can feel it."

With Ava's guidance leading the way, they pressed forward, their footsteps echoing through the maze's twisting corridors. The silence that hung between them was heavy with unspoken tension, each member of the group acutely aware of the stakes that hung in the balance.

As they pushed deeper into the labyrinth's depths, the challenges they faced grew ever more perilous. Deadly traps lay in wait around every corner, their mechanisms designed to ensnare the unwary. Yet, with Ava's sharp mind and Ethan's unwavering leadership, they navigated each obstacle with a combination of skill and determination.

But as they approached the heart of the maze, Ethan could feel a sense of foreboding grip his heart. The air seemed to pulse with a malevolent energy, the darkness thickening around them like a suffocating blanket. They were drawing closer to their final destination, but with each step forward, the danger seemed to grow ever more palpable.

"We must stay focused," Ethan said, his voice low but firm. "We cannot afford to let our guard down now."

With Ava's guidance lighting the way, they pressed on, their determination unwavering in the face of adversity. Liam's usual bravado had returned, his courage bolstered by the knowledge that they were nearing their goal. Maya walked beside Ethan, her eyes fixed on the path ahead, her resolve unshakeable despite the trials they had faced.

As they ventured deeper into the heart of the labyrinth, Ethan could feel the weight of their mission pressing down on him like a leaden cloak. They had come so far, faced countless trials and tribulations, and now, they stood on the brink of the final confrontation.

But as they approached their final destination, Ethan could feel a sense of unease settling over him like a heavy fog. The air seemed to crackle with tension, the darkness closing in around them like a suffocating embrace. They were walking into the lion's den, and with each step forward, the danger seemed to grow ever more palpable.

"We must be prepared for anything," Ethan said, his voice low but firm. "The final confrontation awaits us, and we cannot afford to falter now."

With Ava's guidance lighting the way, they pressed on, their footsteps echoing through the maze's twisting corridors. The silence that hung between them was heavy with unspoken tension, each member of the group acutely aware of the stakes that hung in the balance.

As they ventured deeper into the heart of the labyrinth, Ethan could feel the weight of their mission pressing down on him like a leaden cloak. They had come so far, faced countless trials and tribulations, and now, they stood on the brink of the final confrontation.

But as they approached their final destination, Ethan could feel a sense of unease settling over him like a heavy fog. The air seemed to crackle with tension, the darkness closing in around them like a suffocating embrace. They were walking into the lion's den, and with each step forward, the danger seemed to grow ever more palpable.

"We must be prepared for anything," Ethan said, his voice low but firm. "The final confrontation awaits us, and we cannot afford to falter now."

With Ava's guidance lighting the way, they pressed on, their footsteps echoing through the maze's twisting corridors. The silence that hung between them was heavy with unspoken tension, each member of the group acutely aware of the stakes that hung in the balance.

But as they ventured deeper into the heart of the labyrinth, Ethan could feel a sense of foreboding grip his heart. The air seemed to pulse with a malevolent energy, the darkness thickening around them like a suffocating blanket. They were drawing closer to their final destination, but with each step forward, the danger seemed to grow ever more palpable.

"We must stay focused," Ethan said, his voice low but firm. "We cannot afford to let our guard down now."

With Ava's guidance lighting the way, they pressed on, their determination unwavering in the face of adversity. Liam's usual bravado had returned, his courage bolstered by the knowledge that they were nearing their goal. Maya walked beside Ethan, her eyes fixed on the path ahead, her resolve unshakeable despite the trials they had faced.

As they ventured deeper into the heart of the labyrinth, Ethan could feel the weight of their mission pressing down on him like a leaden cloak. They had come so far, faced countless trials and tribulations, and now, they stood on the brink of the final confrontation.

But as they approached their final destination, Ethan could feel a sense of unease settling over him like a heavy fog. The air seemed to crackle with tension, the darkness closing in around them like a suffocating embrace. They were walking into the lion's den, and with each step forward, the danger seemed to grow ever more palpable.

"We must be prepared for anything," Ethan said, his voice low but firm. "The final confrontation awaits us, and we cannot afford to falter now."

With Ava's guidance lighti

ng the way, they pressed on, looking like the end was near.

CHAPTER SIXTEEN

BEYOND THE WALLS

The final confrontation had left them battered but unbroken, their resolve stronger than ever as they stood on the threshold of the unknown. The labyrinth had been a crucible, forging their bonds and testing their limits, but now, as they gazed out into the vast expanse beyond the walls, Ethan felt a surge of anticipation mingled with apprehension. What lay beyond was a mystery waiting to be unraveled, an adventure waiting to be embraced.

With Ava's strategic guidance lighting the way, they stepped forward into the moonlit landscape, their senses keenly attuned to the unfamiliar sights and sounds that surrounded them. The air was cool and crisp, carrying with it the scent of earth and possibility. Liam's usual bravado had been replaced by a sense of awe, his eyes wide with wonder as he took in the breathtaking panorama before him. Maya walked beside Ethan, her gaze fixed on the horizon, her expression unreadable yet tinged with a hint of excitement.

"We've made it," Ethan whispered, his voice barely audible above the rustle of the wind through the trees. "Beyond the walls, lies freedom."

Their journey had been long and arduous, fraught with peril and uncertainty, but now, as they stood on the precipice of a new beginning, Ethan felt a sense of hope swell within him. They had faced their fears and conquered the challenges that stood in their way, and now, they were ready to embrace whatever lay ahead.

With Ava's guidance leading the way, they ventured further into the untamed wilderness, their footsteps leaving faint impressions in the soft earth beneath them. The world beyond the walls was vast and uncharted, a blank canvas waiting to be explored.

As they journeyed deeper into this new world, they encountered wonders beyond their wildest imagination. Towering mountains rose majestically in the distance, their peaks cloaked in mist. Verdant forests stretched out before them, teeming with life and vitality. And in the distance, the shimmering expanse of a vast ocean beckoned, its siren song calling them forth into the great unknown.

But amidst the beauty and grandeur of their surroundings, Ethan could not shake the feeling of unease that lingered at the edge of his consciousness. They may have escaped the confines of the labyrinth, but their journey was far from over. Dangers still lurked in the shadows, and mysteries still remained unsolved.

With Ava's guidance leading the way, they pressed on, their senses alert for any sign of danger. The world beyond the walls was vast and unpredictable, but with each step forward, Ethan felt a sense of purpose settle over him like a comforting blanket.

They had faced countless challenges together, overcome insurmountable odds, and now, as they stood on the threshold of a new beginning, Ethan knew that whatever trials lay ahead, they would face them together. For in the end, it was their unity, their courage, and their unwavering determination that would see them through.

And as they ventured forth into the unknown, Ethan couldn't help but feel a sense of gratitude for the friends who had stood by his side through it all. They may have escaped the confines of the labyrinth, but their journey was far from over. With Ava's guidance leading the way, they would forge a new path forward, together.

The landscape stretched out before them like a vast, sprawling tapestry, its colors muted in the soft light of the moon. Ethan's senses were overwhelmed by the sheer magnitude of it all, the enormity of the world beyond the walls stretching out before him like a promise waiting to be fulfilled.

With Ava's guidance lighting the way, they pressed forward, their footsteps echoing through the untamed wilderness. Liam's usual bravado had returned, his courage bolstered by the knowledge that they were no longer confined by the constraints of the labyrinth. Maya walked beside Ethan, her eyes scanning the horizon for any sign of danger, her movements fluid and graceful as she navigated the unfamiliar terrain.

As they ventured deeper into the heart of this new world, Ethan felt a sense of wonder and excitement building within him. The possibilities seemed endless, the promise of adventure beckoning to him like a siren's call. They had escaped the confines of the labyrinth, but now, they were faced with a new challenge: forging a path forward in a world that was as beautiful as it was unpredictable.

But amidst the beauty and grandeur of their surroundings, Ethan couldn't shake the feeling of unease that lingered at the edge of his consciousness. They may have escaped the confines of the labyrinth, but their journey was far from over. Dangers still lurked in the shadows, and mysteries still remained unsolved.

With Ava's guidance leading the way, they pressed on, their senses alert for any sign of danger. The world beyond the walls was vast and unpredictable, but with each step forward, Ethan felt a sense of purpose settle over him like a comforting blanket.

They had faced countless challenges together, overcome insurmountable odds, and now, as they stood on the threshold of a new beginning, Ethan knew that whatever trials lay ahead, they would face them together. For in the end, it was their unity, their courage, and their unwavering determination that would see them through.

And as they ventured forth into the unknown, Ethan couldn't help but feel a sense

of gratitude for the friends who had stood by his side through it all. They may have escaped the confines of the labyrinth, but their journey was far from over. With Ava's guidance leading the way, they would forge a new path forward, together.

The landscape stretched out before them like a vast, sprawling tapestry, its colors muted in the soft light of the moon. Ethan's senses were overwhelmed by the sheer magnitude of it all, the enormity of the world beyond the walls stretching out before him like a promise waiting to be fulfilled.

With Ava's guidance lighting the way, they pressed forward, their footsteps echoing through the untamed wilderness. Liam's usual bravado had returned, his courage bolstered by the knowledge that they were no longer confined by the constraints of the labyrinth. Maya walked beside Ethan, her eyes scanning the horizon for any sign of danger, her movements fluid and graceful as she navigated the unfamiliar terrain.

As they ventured deeper into the heart of this new world, Ethan felt a sense of wonder and excitement building within him. The possibilities seemed endless, the promise of adventure beckoning to him like a siren's call. They had escaped the confines of the labyrinth, but now, they were faced with a new challenge: forging a path forward in a world that was as beautiful as it was unpredictable.

But amidst the beauty and grandeur of their surroundings, Ethan couldn't shake the feeling of unease that lingered at the edge of his consciousness. They may have escaped the confines of the labyrinth, but their journey was far from over. Dangers still lurked in the shadows, and mysteries still remained unsolved.

With Ava's guidance leading the way, they pressed on, their senses alert for any sign of danger. The world beyond the walls was vast and unpredictable, but with each step forward, Ethan felt a sense of purpose settle over him like a comforting blanket.

They had faced countless challenges together, overcome insurmountable odds, and now, as they stood on the threshold of a new beginning, Ethan knew that whatever trials lay ahead, they would face them together. For in the end, it was their unity, their courage, and their unwavering determination that would see them through.

And as they ventured forth into the unknown, Ethan couldn't help but feel a sense of gratitude for the friends who had stood by his side through it all. They may have escaped the confines of the labyrinth, but their journey was far from over. With Ava's guidance leading the way, they would forge a new path forward, together.

The landscape stretched out before them like a vast, sprawling tapestry, its colors muted in the soft light of the moon. Ethan's senses were overwhelmed by the sheer magnitude of it all, the enormity of the world beyond the walls stretching out before him like a promise waiting to be fulfilled.

With Ava's guidance lighting the way, they pressed forward, their footsteps echoing through the untamed wilderness. Liam's usual bravado had returned, his courage bolstered by the knowledge that they were no longer confined by the constraints of the labyrinth. Maya walked beside Ethan, her eyes scanning the horizon for any sign of danger, her movements fluid and graceful as she navigated the unfamiliar terrain.

As they ventured deeper into the heart of this new world, Ethan felt a sense of wonder and excitement building within him. The possibilities seemed endless, the promise of adventure beckoning to him like a siren's call. They had escaped the confines of the labyrinth, but now, they were faced with a new challenge: forging a path forward in a world that was as beautiful as it was unpredictable.

But amidst the beauty and grandeur of their surroundings, Ethan couldn't shake the feeling of unease that lingered at the edge of his consciousness. They may have escaped the confines of the labyrinth, but their journey was far from over. Dangers still lurked in the shadows, and mysteries still remained unsolved.

With Ava's guidance leading the way, they pressed on, their senses alert for any sign of danger. The world beyond the walls was vast and unpredictable, but with each step forward, Ethan felt a sense of purpose settle over him like a comforting blanket.

They had faced countless challenges together, overcome insurmountable odds, and now, as they stood on the threshold of a new beginning, Ethan knew that whatever trials lay ahead, they would face them together. For in the end, it was their unity, their courage, and their unwavering determination that would see them through.

And as they ventured forth into the unknown, Ethan couldn't help but feel a sense of gratitude for the friends who had stood by his side through it all. They may have escaped the confines of the labyrinth, but their journey was far from over. With Ava's guidance leading the way, they would forge a new path forward, together.

The landscape stretched out before them like a vast, sprawling tapestry, its colors muted in the soft light of the moon. Ethan's senses were overwhelmed by the sheer magnitude of it all, the enormity of the world beyond the walls stretching out before him like a promise waiting to be fulfilled.

With Ava's guidance lighting the way, they pressed forward, their footsteps echoing through the untamed wilderness. Liam's usual bravado had returned, his courage bolstered by the knowledge that they were no longer confined by the constraints of the labyrinth. Maya walked beside Ethan, her eyes scanning the horizon for any sign of danger, her movements fluid and graceful as she navigated the unfamiliar terrain.

As they ventured deeper into the heart of this new world, Ethan felt a sense

of wonder and excitement building within him. The possibilities seemed endless, the promise of adventure beckoning to him like a siren's call. They had escaped the confines of the labyrinth, but now, they were faced with a new challenge: forging a path forward in a world that was as beautiful as it was unpredictable.

But amidst the beauty and grandeur of their surroundings, Ethan couldn't shake the feeling of unease that lingered at the edge of his consciousness. They may have escaped the confines of the labyrinth, but their journey was far from over. Dangers still lurked in the shadows, and mysteries still remained unsolved.

With Ava's guidance leading the way, they pressed on, their senses alert for any sign of danger. The world beyond the walls was vast and unpredictable, but with each step forward, Ethan felt a sense of purpose settle over him like a comforting blanket.

They had faced countless challenges together, overcome insurmountable odds, and now, as they stood on the threshold of a new beginning, Ethan knew that whatever trials lay ahead, they would face them together. For in the end, it was their unity, their courage, and their unwavering determination that would see them through.

And as they ventured forth into the unknown, Ethan couldn't help but feel a sense of gratitude for the friends who had stood by his side through it all. They may have escaped the confines of the labyrinth, but their journey was far from over. With Ava's guidance leading the way, they would forge a new path forward, together.

The landscape stretched out before them like a vast, sprawling tapestry, its colors muted in the soft light of the moon. Ethan's senses were overwhelmed by the sheer magnitude of it all, the enormity of the world beyond the walls stretching out before him like a promise waiting to be fulfilled.

With Ava's guidance lighting the way, they pressed forward, their footsteps echoing through the untamed wilderness. Liam's usual bravado had returned, his courage bolstered by the knowledge that they were no longer confined by the constraints of the labyrinth. Maya walked beside Ethan, her eyes scanning the horizon for any sign of danger, her movements fluid and graceful as she navigated the unfamiliar terrain.

As they ventured deeper into the heart of this new world, Ethan felt a sense of wonder and excitement building within him. The possibilities seemed endless, the promise of adventure beckoning to him like a siren's call. They had escaped the confines of the labyrinth, but now, they were faced with a new challenge: forging a path forward in a world that was as beautiful as it was unpredictable.

But amidst the beauty and grandeur of their surroundings, Ethan couldn't shake the feeling of unease that lingered at the edge of his consciousness. They may have escaped the confines of the labyrinth, but their journey was far from over. Dangers still lurked in the shadows, and mysteries still remained unsolved.

With Ava's guidance leading the way, they pressed on, their senses alert for any sign of danger. The world beyond the walls was vast and unpredictable, but with each step forward, Ethan felt a sense of purpose settle over him like a comforting blanket.

They had faced countless challenges together, overcome insurmountable odds, and now, as they stood on the threshold of a new beginning, Ethan knew that whatever trials lay ahead, they would face them together. For in the end, it was their unity, their courage, and their unwavering determination that would see them through.

And as they ventured forth into the unknown, Ethan couldn't help but feel a sense of gratitude for the friends who had stood by his side through it all. They may have escaped the confines of the labyrinth, but their journey was far from over. With Ava's guidance leading the way, they would forge a new path forward, together.

The landscape stretched out before them like a vast, sprawling tapestry, its colors muted in the soft light of the moon. Ethan's senses were overwhelmed by the sheer magnitude of it all, the enormity of the world beyond the walls stretching out before him like a promise waiting to be fulfilled.

With Ava's guidance lighting the way, they pressed forward, their footsteps echoing through the untamed wilderness. Liam's usual bravado had returned, his courage bolstered by the knowledge that they were no longer confined by the constraints of the labyrinth. Maya walked beside Ethan, her eyes scanning the horizon for any sign of danger, her movements fluid and graceful as she navigated the unfamiliar terrain.

As they ventured deeper into the heart of this new world, Ethan felt a sense of wonder and excitement building within him. The possibilities seemed endless, the promise of adventure beckoning to him like a siren's call. They had escaped the confines of the labyrinth, but now, they were faced with a new challenge: forging a path forward in a world that was as beautiful as it was unpredictable.

But amidst the beauty and grandeur of their surroundings, Ethan couldn't shake the feeling of unease that lingered at the edge of his consciousness. They may have escaped the confines of the labyrinth, but their journey was far from over. Dangers still lurked in the shadows, and mysteries still remained unsolved.

With Ava's guidance leading the way, they pressed on, their senses alert for any sign of danger. The world beyond the walls was vast and unpredictable, but with each step forward, Ethan felt a sense of purpose settle over him like a comforting blanket.

They had faced countless challenges together, overcome insurmountable odds, and now, as they stood on the threshold of a new beginning, Ethan knew that whatever trials lay ahead, they would face them together. For in t

he end, it was their unity, their courage, and their unwavering determination that would see them through.

CHAPTER SEVENTEEN

THE VIRAL PLAGUE

The team found temporary solace within the confines of a secluded chamber, their weary bodies seeking respite from the relentless trials of the labyrinth. As they settled down, exhaustion weighed heavy on their shoulders, but their guard remained high, ever vigilant against the dangers that lurked in the shadows.

Ava's curiosity led her to a peculiar display screen nestled in the corner of the chamber. With a hesitant press, the screen flickered to life, casting an eerie glow across the room. What they witnessed on the screen sent shivers down their spines—footage of the viral outbreak that had plunged their world into chaos.

Images of panic and devastation played out before them, the streets overrun by hordes of infected individuals. The virus had spread rapidly, leaving destruction in its wake. As they watched in grim silence, a sudden commotion outside shattered the fragile peace of the chamber.

Without warning, the chamber was besieged by a horde of infected, their eyes vacant, their movements erratic and aggressive. The team sprang into action, weapons drawn, as they fought desperately to defend themselves against the onslaught.

The infected lunged forward with frenzied determination, their movements jerky and unpredictable. Ethan swung his weapon with precision, fending off their relentless attacks as best he could. Ava, Liam, and Maya fought alongside him, their movements fluid and coordinated as they worked together to repel the advancing horde.

But the infected were relentless, their numbers seemingly endless. With each passing moment, the team grew more fatigued, their energy waning as the battle raged on. Despite their valiant efforts, the infected pressed on, overwhelming them with sheer numbers.

As the fight wore on, Ethan couldn't help but notice the symptoms of the virus manifesting in the infected individuals. Their skin was pallid and clammy, their eyes vacant and glassy. Some exhibited signs of physical decay, their bodies ravaged by the effects of the virus.

But it was their behavior that was most unsettling—erratic and unpredictable, driven by an insatiable hunger for flesh. It was clear that they were no longer human, mere shells of their former selves consumed by the viral plague that ravaged their minds and bodies.

Just as the team began to falter under the relentless assault, a second wave of infected surged forth, even more ferocious than the last. With their backs against the wall, the team fought with renewed determination, pushing themselves to their limits as they battled against overwhelming odds.

But just when all hope seemed lost, a figure emerged from the shadows, wielding a weapon with deadly precision. With swift and decisive movements, they fought alongside the team, driving back the tide of infected with unparalleled skill and determination.

Their arrival was a beacon of hope in the darkness, a glimmer of light amidst the chaos. And as the last of the infected fell, Ethan turned to their savior, gratitude shining in his eyes.

"Thank you," he said, his voice filled with sincerity. "We wouldn't have survived without your help."

The stranger offered a solemn nod, their expression unreadable. "No thanks are necessary," they replied, their voice tinged with a hint of sadness. "I only did what needed to be done."

As the team regrouped and prepared to continue their journey through the labyrinth, Ethan couldn't help but feel a sense of gratitude for their mysterious benefactor. With renewed resolve, they pressed forward, ready to confront whatever trials awaited them in the depths of the labyrinth.

The Forbidden Odyssey

Book#2

It is the story is place somewhere before the event of
Labyrinth of Abyss.

It answers how to virus was made and about the world they
used to know, Construction of Enigma and the stranger at the end.

*Detective Nick Howler and his colleagues were sent to investigate
the mystery of the Lost caves.*

*Two criminals, one a thief and other a mad scientist, escaped the
prison...*

*What was the mystery of the Lost caves? Is it a conspiracy or a
false theory.*

Stay tuned for the next adventure of the tale before the
Enigma.